★STUDY GUIDES

Mathematics

Year 4

Jenny Lawson

RISING ★ STARS

Rising Stars UK Ltd, 7 Hatchers Mews, Bermondsey Street, London SE1 3GS

www.risingstars-uk.com

Every effort has been made to trace copyright holders and obtain their permission for the use of copyright materials. The authors and publisher will gladly receive information enabling them to rectify any error or omission in subsequent editions.

All facts are correct at time of going to press.

Published 2007
Reprinted 2009, 2011
Text, design and layout © Rising Stars UK Ltd.

Design: HL Studios and Clive Sutherland
Illustrations: Oxford Designers and Illustrators
Editorial project management: Dodi Beardshaw
Editorial: Joanne Osborn
Cover design: Burville-Riley Partnership

British Library Cataloguing in Publication Data.
A CIP record for this book is available from the British Library.

ISBN: 978-1-84680-100-6

Printed by Craft Print International Ltd, Singapore

Contents

How to get the best out of this book

Each chapter spreads across two pages. All chapters focus on one topic and should help you to keep 'On track' and to 'Aim higher'.

Title: tells you the topic for the chapter.

What do you need to know? and **What will you learn?** tell you what you need to know before you start this chapter and what you are aiming to learn from this chapter.

Key facts: set out what you need to know and the ideas you need to understand fully.

Key words and their meanings: help to build up your mathematical vocabulary. Remember that some words mean one thing in everyday life and something more special in Mathematics.

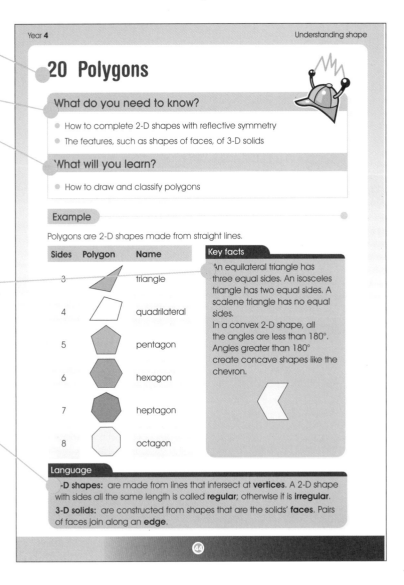

Year **4**   Understanding shape

20 Polygons

What do you need to know?

- How to complete 2-D shapes with reflective symmetry
- The features, such as shapes of faces, of 3-D solids

What will you learn?

- How to draw and classify polygons

Example

Polygons are 2-D shapes made from straight lines.

Sides	Polygon	Name
3		triangle
4		quadrilateral
5		pentagon
6		hexagon
7		heptagon
8		octagon

Key facts

An equilateral triangle has three equal sides. An isosceles triangle has two equal sides. A scalene triangle has no equal sides.
In a convex 2-D shape, all the angles are less than 180°. Angles greater than 180° create concave shapes like the chevron.

Language

-D shapes: are made from lines that intersect at **vertices**. A 2-D shape with sides all the same length is called **regular**; otherwise it is **irregular**.
3-D solids: are constructed from shapes that are the solids' **faces**. Pairs of faces join along an **edge**.

44

Follow these simple rules if you are using the book for revising.

1 Read each page carefully. Give yourself time to take in each idea.

2 Learn the key facts and ideas. Ask your teacher or mum, dad or the adult who looks after you if you need help.

3 Concentrate on the things you find more difficult.

4 Only work for about 20 minutes or so at a time. Take a break and then do more work.

If you get most of the **On track** questions right then you know you are working at level 3 or 4. Well done – that's brilliant! If you get most of the **Aiming higher** questions right, you are working at the higher level 4. You're doing really well!

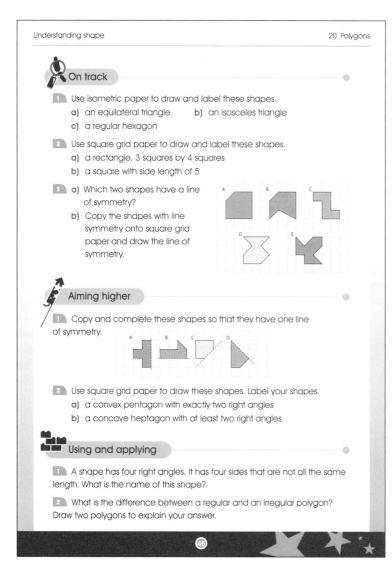

The **Using and applying** questions are often more challenging and ask you to explain your answers or think of different ways of answering. These questions will be around level 4 or above.

Some questions must be answered without using a calculator – look for [icon]. If you are not using a calculator be sure to write down the calculations you are doing. If you are using a calculator remember to try to check your answer to see if it is sensible.

Follow these simple rules if you want to know how well you are doing.

1 Work through the questions.

2 Keep a record of how well you do.

3 If you are working at level 3 you will get most of the **On track** questions correct.

4 If you are working at level 4 you will also get most of the **Aiming higher** questions correct.

1 Number sequences

What do you need to know?

- How to count on from zero and back to zero in single-digit steps or multiples of 10

What will you learn?

- How to recognise number sequences
- How to continue these number sequences

Example

A simple type of sequence is one that obeys a rule such as 'add 4'.

add 4   add 4   add 4   add 4   add 4

2   6   10   14   18   ...

Notice the constant difference of 4 between each pair of terms in the sequence.

$6 - 2 = 4$ $10 - 6 = 4$ $14 - 10 = 4$ $18 - 14 = 4$

Here is another sequence: 18, 15, 12, 9, 6. What is the rule? Notice that the numbers get smaller, so the rule is 'subtract something'. To decide on the rule, work out the difference between each pair of terms in the sequence.

$18 - 15 = 3$ $15 - 12 = 3$ $12 - 9 = 3$ $9 - 6 = 3$

- *The difference is 3, so the rule is 'subtract 3'.*

Key facts

A number sequence starts with a number and then a rule tells you how to work out all the numbers that follow.

Language

Sequence: a list of numbers created to follow a rule.

Constant: a number that does not change.

Rule: this tells you what to do. For example, 'add 4' or 'subtract 1'.

On track

1 The rule for a sequence is 'count on in threes'. The first number in the sequence is 10. Write down the next two numbers in the sequence.

2 A number sequence starts with 10. The rule is 'count back in twos'. Write down the next two numbers in the sequence.

3 What is the rule for making numbers in this sequence?

..., ..., 10, 12, 14, ..., ...

Fill in the missing numbers in this sequence.

Aiming higher

1 These two number sequences are made using the same rule.

36, 44, 52, 60, ...   76, 84, 92, 100, ...

What is the rule? Write down the next two numbers in each sequence.

2 Which of these number sequences has the number 40 in it?

a) 3, 6, 9, 12, ...   **b)** 4, 8, 12, 16, ...   **c)** 5, 10, 15, 20, ...

Explain your answer.

Using and applying

1 Anil and Bala are playing a counting-on game. Anil counts up in fours and starts on zero. Bala counts up in twos and starts on 10. They take it in turns to call out a number in their sequence.

0, 4, 8, ...   10, 12, 14, ...

Anil starts first.

Who was the first to say 32? Show how you worked out your answer.

2 Lisa went on holiday. In five days, she made 40 sandcastles.

Each day she made four fewer castles than the day before.

How many sandcastles did she make on the fifth day?

2 Comparing numbers

What do you need to know?

- How to partition and round 3-digit numbers into multiples of 1, 10 and 100

What will you learn?

- How to partition, round and order 4-digit whole numbers
- About negative numbers and where they lie on a number line
- How to use the symbols < and > to compare numbers

Example

You can partition 4-digit numbers just like 2-digit and 3-digit numbers.

$$15 = 10 + 5 \qquad 263 = 200 + 60 + 3 \qquad 4918 = 4000 + 900 + 10 + 8$$

A 3-digit number can be rounded to the nearest 10 or 100, but a 4-digit number can also be rounded to the nearest 1000.

4918 is 4900 to the nearest 100   4918 is 4920 to the nearest 10   4918 is 5000 to the nearest 1000

4900 4910 4920 4930 4940 4950 4960 4970 4980 4990 5000

4918

Key facts

The number line can be extended back beyond zero.

negative numbers   zero   positive numbers

−6   −2   0   2   3   5   7   10

When numbers are not equal, a less than symbol (<) or greater than symbol (>) can show which is smaller and which is bigger.

$$2 < 5 \qquad 5 > 2 \qquad 7 > 3 \qquad -10 < 0 \qquad -2 > -6$$

$2 < 5$ says the same as $5 > 2$. Although $2 < 6$, $-6 < -2$.

In a 4-digit number, the 1st digit is the number of thousands, the 2nd the number of hundreds, the 3rd the number of tens, the 4th digit the number of units. To order numbers, look at the 1st digit first, then the 2nd digit, and so on.

Language

Positive number: above zero.   **Negative number:** below zero.

On track

1. Copy and complete these number sentences.

   a) $20\boxed{}3 = 2000 + 40 + 3$ b) $3017 = \boxed{} + 10 + 7$

2. Fill in the missing numbers on this part of the number line.

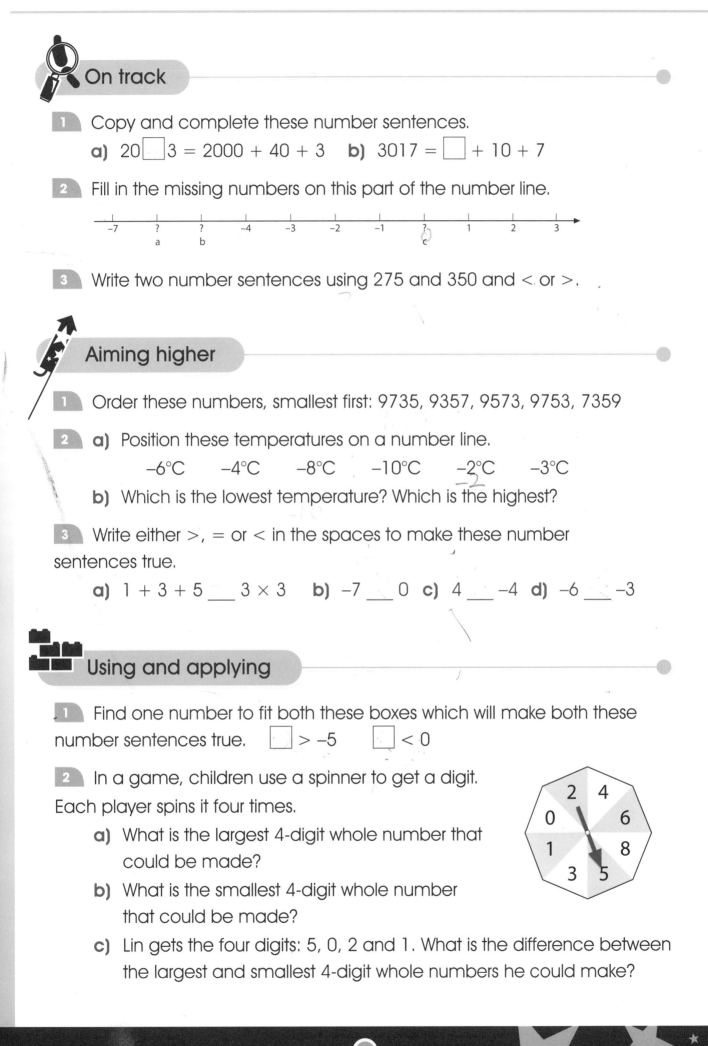

3. Write two number sentences using 275 and 350 and < or >.

Aiming higher

1. Order these numbers, smallest first: 9735, 9357, 9573, 9753, 7359

2. a) Position these temperatures on a number line.

      −6°C   −4°C   −8°C   −10°C   −2°C   −3°C

   b) Which is the lowest temperature? Which is the highest?

3. Write either >, = or < in the spaces to make these number sentences true.

   a) $1 + 3 + 5$ ___ 3×3 b) -7 ___ 0 c) 4 ___ -4 d) -6 ___ -3

Using and applying

1. Find one number to fit both these boxes which will make both these number sentences true. $\boxed{} > -5$ $\boxed{} < 0$

2. In a game, children use a spinner to get a digit. Each player spins it four times.

   a) What is the largest 4-digit whole number that could be made?

   b) What is the smallest 4-digit whole number that could be made?

   c) Lin gets the four digits: 5, 0, 2 and 1. What is the difference between the largest and smallest 4-digit whole numbers he could make?

3 Tenths and hundredths

What do you need to know?

- How to position whole numbers up to 1000 on a number line
- How to write money amounts using £ and p notation

What will you learn?

- How to use decimal notation for tenths and hundredths
- How to recognise tenths and hundredths in money and measurements
- How to position 1- and 2-place decimal numbers on a number line

Example

In a whole number, the position of a digit tells you its place value. In 352, the 3 is worth 300 and the 5 is worth 50. In a decimal number, a decimal point separates the whole number part from the digits that represent tenths and hundredths and other smaller values.

```
H T U . t h
3 5 2 . 4 7
```

In 352.47, the 4 is worth four tenths. The 7 is worth seven hundredths.

In £352.47, the 4 represents 40p and the 7 represents 7p.

Key facts

A tenth is what you get when you divide something into ten parts. It is ten times smaller than a unit (or whole).

A hundredth is what you get when you divide something into 100 parts. It is ten times smaller than a tenth and 100 times smaller than a unit (or whole).

Language

Place value: the value of a digit according to the column it is in.

Decimal: a system of counting that uses ten digits: 0, 1, 2, 3, 4, 5, 6, 7, 8 and 9.

On track

1 Copy and complete these.
a) 61.9 is ... tens + ... unit + ... tenths
b) 35.72 is ... tens + ... units + ... tenths + ... hundredths

2 Write down what the digit 3 represents in each of these.
a) £135 b) £15.30 c) £31.50 d) £15.03 e) £3105

3 Write down what the digit 1 represents in each of these.
a) 4.1 m b) 5.01 m c) 61 m d) 0.71 m

4 Draw a number line from 3 to 5 and show these numbers on it.
a) 3.1 b) 3.5 c) 3.9 d) 4.25

Aiming higher

1 Put each of these amounts of money in order, smallest first.
£0.06 £600 £6 £0.60 £60

2 Put these measurements in order of length, longest first.
23 m 2.1 m 230 cm 22.5 m

Using and applying

1 Five books cost £23. Karl worked out the cost of one book. His calculator showed 4.6. What did one book cost?

2 Here are the long jump distances by women athletes at the 2004 Paralympics in Athens.
a) Who won? b) How many of the women jumped over 4.5 m?

Name	Distance (m)	Name	Distance (m)
Guilhermino	3.75	Martinez	4.93
Ivekovic	5.31	Martinez, Maria	4.67
Kannus	5.03	Miao Miao	5.20
Kanuik	5.48	Yang	4.87
Knors	4.77	Zinkevich	5.66
Lazaro	5.63		

4 Decimals and fractions

What do you need to know?

- How to read and write simple fractions

What will you learn?

- That $\frac{1}{2} = \underline{0.5}$, $\frac{1}{4} = \underline{0.25}$, $\frac{3}{4} = \underline{0.75}$, $\frac{1}{10} = \underline{0.1}$ and $\frac{1}{100} = \underline{0.01}$

Example

$\frac{1}{2} = \frac{5}{10} = 0.5$

$\frac{1}{4} = \frac{25}{100} = 0.25$

$\frac{3}{4} = \frac{75}{100} = 0.75$

Key facts

If the numerator is smaller than the denominator, the fraction is less than 1.
If the numerator is the same as the denominator, the fraction is equivalent to 1.

Language

Fraction: a fraction is written with one number on the top (numerator) and one number on the bottom (denominator).

On track

1 Write one-half as a fraction and as a decimal.

2 Write one-quarter as a fraction and as a decimal.

3 Write three-quarters as a fraction and as a decimal.

4 Which of these is the same as 0.3?

a) three   **b)** three-tenths   **c)** three-hundredths   **d)** one-third

5 Which of these fractions is the same as nought point four?

$$\frac{1}{4} \qquad \frac{1}{40} \qquad \frac{1}{400} \qquad \frac{4}{10} \qquad \frac{4}{100}$$

6 Which of these decimals means $\frac{7}{10}$?

70   7   0.7   0.07

Aiming higher

1 Write two fractions that are the same as 0.5.

2 Write two fractions that are the same as 0.25.

3 How many hundredths are the same as 0.25?

4 How many pence are the same as £0.25?

5 How many centimetres are the same as 0.75 m?

Using and applying

1 You have measured this pencil.
Write its length as a decimal and
then as a fraction.

2 You have been using your calculator to find an answer.
The display reads 1.25. What could this mean?
Write a story to explain the calculation you have done.

5 Equivalent fractions

What do you need to know?

- How to use diagrams to compare fractions and to find equivalent fractions

What will you learn?

- How to use diagrams to find equivalent fractions

Example

These fractions are all equivalent to $\frac{1}{3}$.

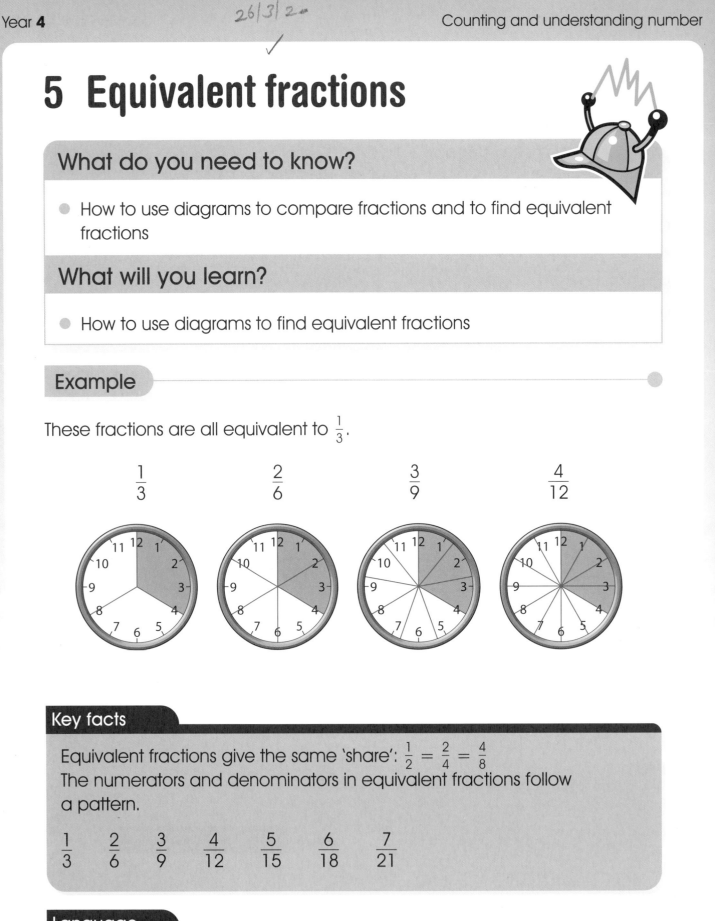

$$\frac{1}{3} \qquad \frac{2}{6} \qquad \frac{3}{9} \qquad \frac{4}{12}$$

Key facts

Equivalent fractions give the same 'share': $\frac{1}{2} = \frac{2}{4} = \frac{4}{8}$
The numerators and denominators in equivalent fractions follow a pattern.

$$\frac{1}{3} \qquad \frac{2}{6} \qquad \frac{3}{9} \qquad \frac{4}{12} \qquad \frac{5}{15} \qquad \frac{6}{18} \qquad \frac{7}{21}$$

Language

Numerator: the top number in a fraction.

Denominator: the bottom number in a fraction.

Equivalent: the same as.

On track

1 What fraction of these squirrels is grey?

2 Which two of these shapes have three-quarters shaded? Explain how you know.

a)   b)   c)   d)   e)

Aiming higher

1 What fraction of this shape is shaded? Write your answer in two different ways.

$\frac{2}{8}$

$\frac{1}{4}$

2 Write two fractions that are equivalent to ¼. $\frac{2}{8}\frac{4}{16}$

3 Write two fractions that are equivalent to ⁴⁄₉.

Using and applying

1 The pizza was sliced into six equal slices. I ate two of the slices. What fraction of the pizza did I eat? $\frac{2}{6}$

2 I ate more than ½ a pizza but less than ¾. What fraction could I have eaten? $\frac{5}{8}$

— 4¼

3 What would you prefer: three pizzas shared between four people, or five pizzas shared between six people? Explain why. 5 pizzas shared b

— 6

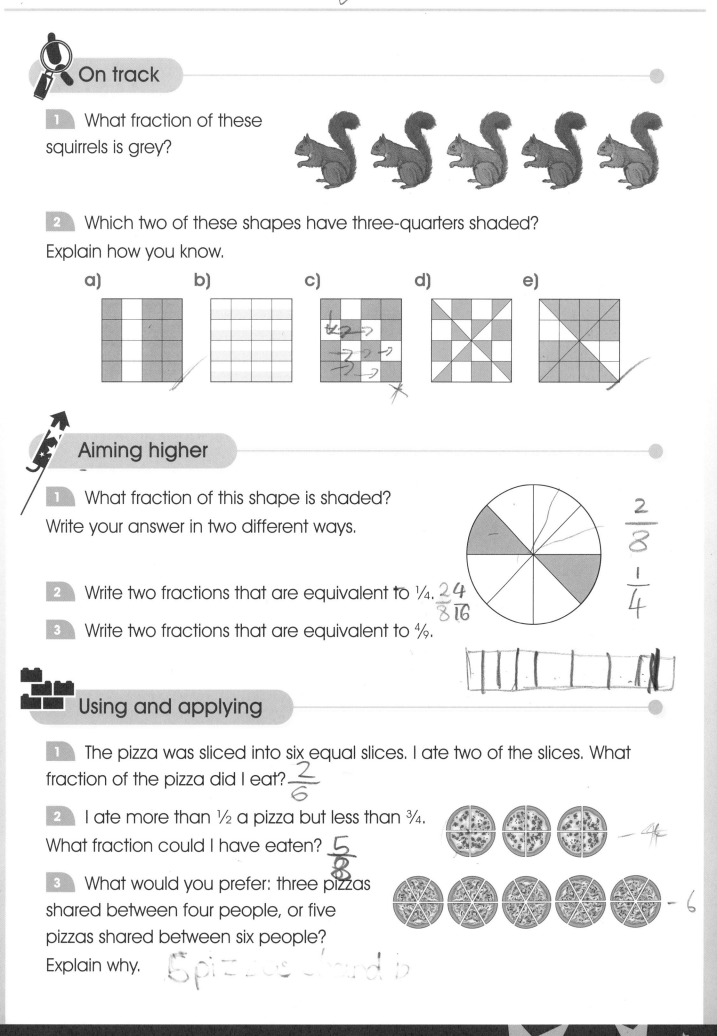

6 Mixed numbers

What do you need to know?

- How to position whole numbers and 1- and 2-place decimal numbers on a number line

What will you learn?

- To interpret mixed numbers and position them on a number line

Example

When the numerator of a fraction is bigger than the denominator, the fraction is top-heavy. $\frac{3}{2}$ $\frac{4}{3}$ $\frac{6}{5}$ $\frac{9}{8}$

Top-heavy fractions that have 1 as the denominator can be written as whole numbers. $\frac{2}{1} = 2$ $\frac{4}{1} = 4$

Other top-heavy fractions can be written as mixed numbers.

$$\frac{5}{4} = \frac{4+1}{4} = 1 + \frac{1}{4} = 1\frac{1}{4}$$

Top-heavy fractions appear to the right of 1 on the number line.

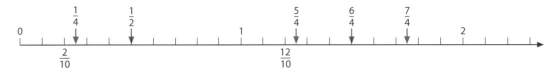

Key facts

Mixed numbers can be written using a proper fraction for the fractional part, or as a decimal.

$1.01 = 1\frac{1}{100}$ $2.1 = 2\frac{1}{10}$ $3.25 = 3\frac{1}{4}$ $4.5 = 4\frac{1}{2}$ $5.75 = 5\frac{3}{4}$

Language

Mixed number: like $1\frac{1}{2}$, a whole number part (the 1) and a fractional part (the $\frac{1}{2}$).

On track

1. Convert these fractions into whole numbers.

   a) $\frac{9}{1}$ b) $\frac{7}{1}$ c) $\frac{5}{1}$

2. Which of these are top-heavy fractions?

   a) $\frac{2}{3}$ b) $\frac{7}{6}$ c) $\frac{5}{9}$ d) $\frac{8}{5}$ e) $\frac{3}{4}$ f) $\frac{6}{4}$

3. Draw a number line from 0 to 3. Label it to show a fraction:

   a) that is bigger than $\frac{1}{2}$ but smaller than 1

   b) that is bigger than 1 but smaller than 2

   c) that is bigger than 2 but smaller than 3.

Aiming higher

1. Write these fractions as mixed numbers with fractional parts.

   a) $\frac{3}{2}$ b) $\frac{4}{3}$ c) $\frac{6}{5}$ d) $\frac{9}{8}$ e) $\frac{7}{4}$ f) $\frac{11}{10}$

2. Write these fractions as mixed numbers in decimal form.

   a) $\frac{5}{4}$ b) $\frac{7}{4}$ c) $\frac{11}{10}$ d) $\frac{101}{100}$ e) $\frac{125}{100}$ f) $\frac{25}{20}$ g) $\frac{40}{25}$ h) $\frac{110}{50}$

3. Write these mixed numbers as top-heavy fractions.

   a) $1\frac{1}{5}$ b) $2\frac{1}{4}$ c) $3\frac{1}{3}$ d) $4\frac{1}{2}$

Using and applying

1. Amy wants to cut a piece of ribbon $1\frac{3}{4}$ cm long. Where she should cut it?

2. Brian is counting in quarters. Fill in the gaps for him.

   $\frac{1}{4}$ $\frac{1}{2}$ $\frac{3}{4}$ 1   ☐ $1\frac{1}{2}$ $1\frac{3}{4}$ ☐

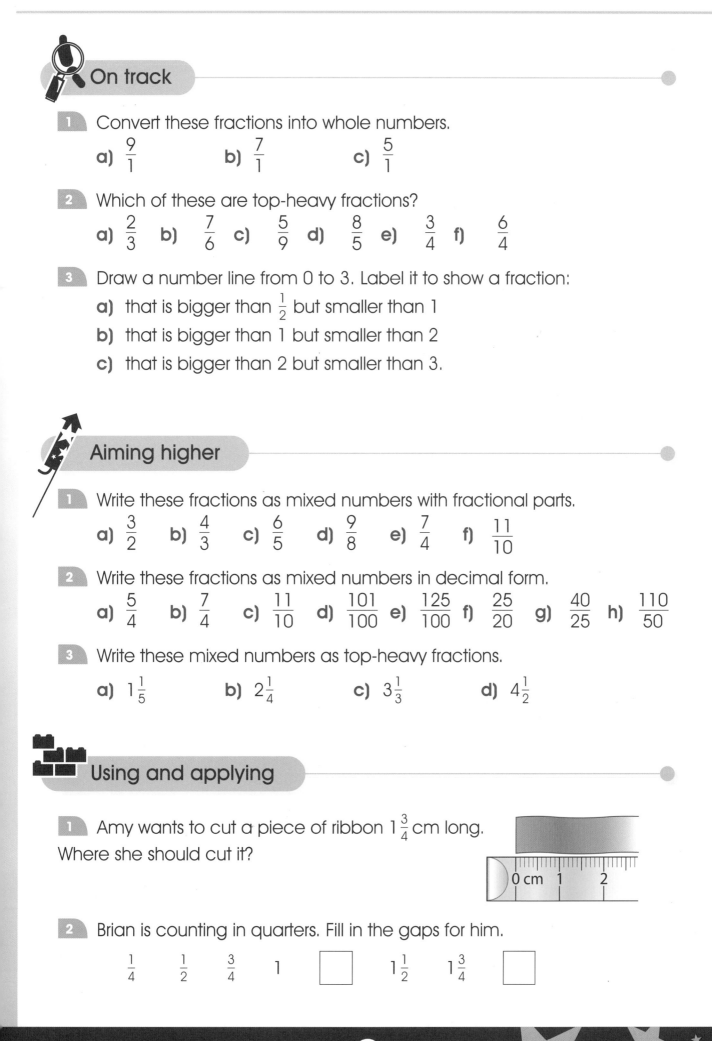

7 Ratio and proportion

What do you need to know?

- How to estimate small numbers of objects
- How to draw a fraction diagram

What will you learn?

- How to use the phrases 'in every' and 'for every'
- How to estimate a proportion

Example

Look at this pattern. How would you describe the proportion of red and blue squares?

- *There is one red square in every four squares.* $\frac{1}{4}$ *of the squares are red.*
- *There is one red square for every three blue squares.* $\frac{3}{4}$ *of the squares are blue.*

Guess the proportion of blue and green pencils.

- *There are about three times as many green pencils as blue. It looks like for every blue pencil, there are three green pencils.*

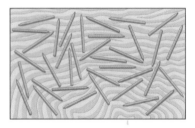

Key facts

When talking about ratios, the order matters. 'Two red squares for every three green triangles' is not the same as 'Three red squares for every two green triangles'.

Language

The terms **'for every'** and **'in every'** can be used to describe proportions.

On track

1   When full, these jars can each hold 100 marbles. How many marbles do you think there are in each jar?

a)   b)   c)   d)

2   Which of these diagrams has three out of every four squares shaded?

a)   b)   c)   d)

3   To every square there are four sides. How many sides are there in five squares?

Aiming higher

1   a) Copy and complete this sentence:
        For every ... blue pencil, there are ...
        red pencils.

   b) What proportion of the pencils is blue?
        What proportion of the pencils is red?

   c) Add your answers to part b) together.
        What do you get?

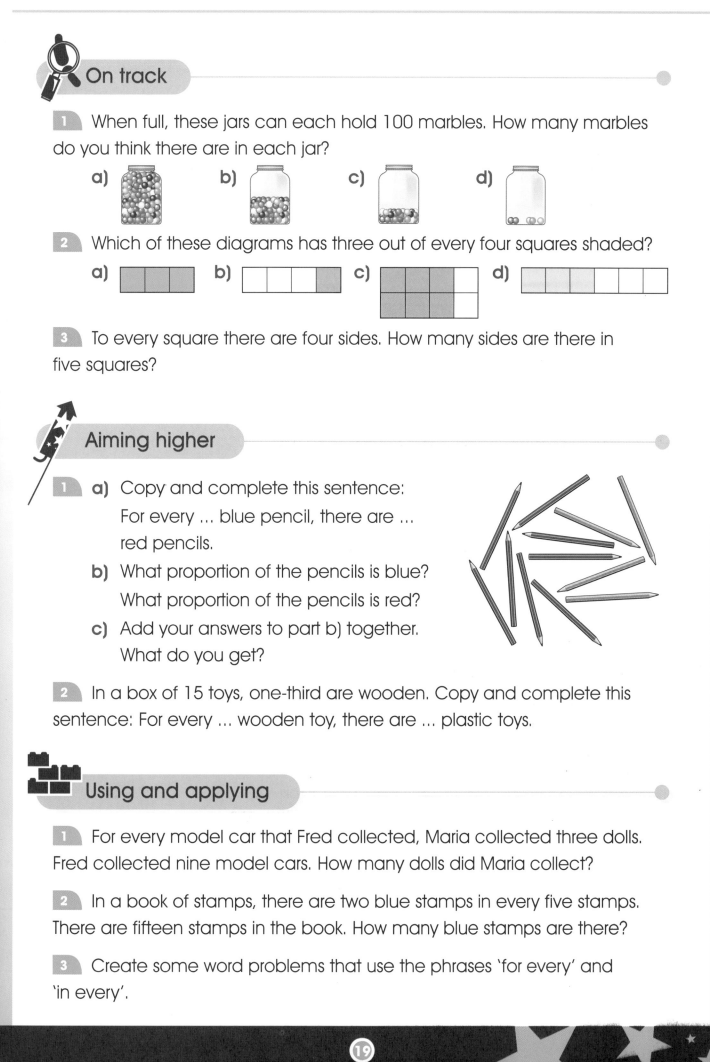

2   In a box of 15 toys, one-third are wooden. Copy and complete this sentence: For every ... wooden toy, there are ... plastic toys.

Using and applying

1   For every model car that Fred collected, Maria collected three dolls. Fred collected nine model cars. How many dolls did Maria collect?

2   In a book of stamps, there are two blue stamps in every five stamps. There are fifteen stamps in the book. How many blue stamps are there?

3   Create some word problems that use the phrases 'for every' and 'in every'.

8 Addition and subtraction facts

What do you need to know?

- All addition and subtraction facts for each number to 20
- All sums and differences of multiples of 10
- All number pairs that total 100

What will you learn?

- How to use addition and subtraction facts to calculate sums and differences for pairs of multiples of 10, 100 or 1000

Example

To calculate a sum like:	$30 + 80$	
Use an addition fact like:	$3 + 8 = 11$	$30 + 80 = 110$
It also works for bigger numbers:		$300 + 800 = 1100$
And even bigger numbers:		$3000 + 8000 = 11,000$

To calculate a difference like:	$70 - 50$	
Use a subtraction fact like:	$7 - 5 = 2$	$70 - 50 = 20$
This also works for bigger numbers:		$700 - 500 = 200$
		$7000 - 5000 = 2000$

Key facts

In 7000, the digit 7 stands for seven thousand. The three zeros are placeholders to show no hundreds, no tens and no units.

Language

Sum: the sum of two numbers is what you get when you add them.

Difference: the difference of two numbers is what you get if you subtract the smaller one from the bigger one.

Placeholder: a zero that shows there is no value for that column of the number.

On track

1   Copy and fill the gaps: 4 + 8 = 12 so 40 + 80 = … and 400 + 800 = …

+	40	…	30	…
20	60	…	…	110
80	…	100	…	170
10	50	30	…	100
…	…	90	…	160

2   Copy and complete this addition grid.

Aiming higher

1   Copy and complete this magic square.

40	…	80
…	50	10
20	…	60

2   Use these number cards to make up as many additions as you can that have an answer of 1000.

Here is one way: 100 + 400 + 500

Using and applying

1   A cinema has three screens, seating 200, 300 and 500 people. What is the total number of seats?

2   This table shows the number of people allowed at sports stadiums.

Stadium	No. of people allowed
Bloomfield Road	9000
Field Mill	10,000
Gateshead International	12,000
Holker Street	5000
Meadow Park	4000
Rockingham Triangle	3000
The Shay	14,000

a)   How many more people are allowed into Bloomfield Road than into the Rockingham Triangle?

b)   What is the total number of people allowed into Gateshead International and Holker Street?

9 Doubles and halves

What do you need to know?

- Doubles of all numbers to 20 and halves of all even numbers to 40

What will you learn?

- How to identify doubles of 2-digit numbers
- How to calculate doubles and halves of multiples of 10 and 100

Example

Here is one way to work out double 36. Partition the 36 so that each part has only a single non-zero digit: $36 = 30 + 6$

Then do the multiplication on each digit, separately:

$$2 \times 36 = 2 \times 30 + 2 \times 6 = 60 + 12 = 72$$

To calculate doubles of multiples of 10 and 100, remember to preserve the placeholder zeros:

$$2 \times 360 = 720 \qquad 2 \times 3600 = 7200$$

To halve a number, you may need to partition the number first:

$$690 = 600 + 80 + 10$$
$$690 \div 2 = 300 + 40 + 5 = 345$$

Key facts

Halving and doubling are inverse operations. Doubling is the same as multiplying by 2. Halving is the same as dividing by 2.

Language

Inverse operations: inverse operations 'undo' each other.

Partitioned: a number is partitioned by breaking it into smaller numbers. This can be done in many ways, e.g. $57 = 50 + 7 = 40 + 17$.

On track

1. Copy and find the missing numbers.

   a) $15 \times 2 = \square$
   b) $\boxed{16} \div 2 = 80$
   c) $60 \times \square = 120$
   d) $\square \times 2 = 84$
   e) $120 \div 2 = \square$
   f) $180 \div \square = 90$

2. These number sequences are made by doubling the number that goes before. Write down the next three numbers in each sequence.

   a) 1, 2, 4, 8, 16, 32, ..., ..., ...   b) 30, 60, 120, ..., ..., ...

Aiming higher

1. Miki is playing a computer game about doubling numbers.

Maths Zone - Doubling
Doubling Numbers up to 100
1. Double 25 ? 54
2. Double 16 ? 31
3. Double 27 ? 44
4. Double 35 ? 70
5. Double 36 ? 71

   Correct the ones he has got wrong.

2. Amy wants to find out how many times she must keep doubling, starting from 5, to get to over 1000. Here is her working so far.

   $5 \rightarrow 10 \rightarrow 20 \rightarrow 40 \rightarrow$

   Carry on her working until you get to over 1000. How many times does Amy have to double?

Using and applying

1. There are 28 pupils in class 4A. Half the pupils in 4A have a mobile phone. How many pupils in 4A have a mobile phone?

2. Jade was given £10 for her birthday. Amber was given twice as much for her birthday. How much did Amber get for her birthday?

3. There are 420 pupils in a school. Half the pupils come to school by bus. How many pupils come to school by bus?

4. Jen is twice as old as her brother Richard. Jen is 10 years old. How old is her brother Richard?

5. Explain how you work out 260×2 when you know that $26 \times 2 = 52$. Use your method to work out 2600×2.

10 Multiplication and division facts

What do you need to know?

- The 2, 3, 4, 5, 6 and 10 times tables

What will you learn?

- Multiplication facts and matching division facts up to 10 x 10
- Multiples of numbers up to 10 to the tenth multiple

Example

You already know multiplication facts like 4×7, 5×8 and 2×9. Learning the 7, 8 and 9 times tables only means learning six new number facts.

$\times$	7	8	9
7	49	56	63
8	56	64	72
9	63	72	81

Then you can learn their matching division facts:

$49 \div 7 = 7$ $56 \div 7 = 8$ $63 \div 7 = 9$

$56 \div 8 = 7$ $64 \div 8 = 8$ $72 \div 8 = 9$

$63 \div 9 = 7$ $72 \div 9 = 8$ $81 \div 9 = 9$

The multiples of 7 are the 7 times table: 7, 14, 21, 28, 35, 42, 49, 56, 63 and 70.

Key facts

For each multiplication fact like:	$7 \times 9 = 63$
there is another multiplication fact:	$9 \times 7 = 63$
For each multiplication fact like:	$7 \times 9 = 63$
there are two division facts:	$63 \div 7 = 9$ $63 \div 9 = 7$

Language

Remainder: what's left over when you divide by a number that doesn't 'go exactly'.

On track

1. Which of these numbers divide by 4 with no remainder?
   a) 36   b) 63   c) 14   d) 41   e) 22   f) 28

2. Which of these divisions give a remainder of 3?
   a) $13 \div 6$ b) $23 \div 3$ c) $23 \div 4$ d) $33 \div 6$
   e) $33 \div 10$ f) $43 \div 5$

3. How many sevens are there in 49?

4. Share 64 between 8.

5. Which number divided by 8 gives an answer of 9?

Aiming higher

1. Copy these and fill in the missing numbers.
   a) $\square \times 9 = 63$ b) $\square \times 8 = 72$ c) $\square \times 7 = 49$
   d) $90 = 10 \times \square$ e) $8 \times \square = 64$ f) $7 \times \square = 56$

2. Write the multiples of 8, up to the tenth multiple.

3. Write the multiples of 9, up to the tenth multiple.

4. Which number appears in your answers to both questions 3 and 4? Explain why.

Using and applying

1. A coach has 9 rows of seats for passengers. There are 6 seats in each row. How many passengers can the minibus carry?

2. How many egg boxes, each holding 6 eggs, can be filled by 48 eggs?

3. Jill saves 90p of her pocket money each week. How much has she saved after 7 weeks?

4. Seven friends share £56. How much do they each get?

5. James puts 42 stickers in a book. There is space for 9 stickers on a page. How many pages does he use?

11 Using rounding

What do you need to know?

- How to round numbers less than 1000 to the nearest 10 or 100

What will you learn?

- How to use rounding to estimate and check calculations

Example

When you round to the nearest 10, the rounded number has a 0 in the unit column. To decide what goes in the tens column look at the units figure.

HTU	HTU	
13**7** ↑ 140		If the units figure is 5 or above, round up.
13**4** ↓ 130		If the units figure is less than 5, round down.

When you round to the nearest 100, the rounded number has 0 in the tens and unit columns. To decide what to put in the hundreds column look at the tens figure.

HTU	HTU	
3**7**2 ↑ 400		If the tens figure is 5 or above, round up.
3**4**7 ↓ 300		If the tens figure is less than 5, round down.

How can you use rounding to check an answer to a question like: $9 \times 19 = ?$

- *$10 \times 20 = 200$ so any answer that is very different from 200 is wrong.*
- *$9 \times 9 = 81$, so you'd expect the answer to have a 1 in the units column.*

Key facts

Rounding lets you create an approximation to an answer before you do the actual calculation. If the calculated answer is very different to the estimate then you have made a mistake.

Language

Rounding up: goes up to the next unit or 10 or 100.
Rounding down: goes down to the previous unit or 10 or 100.

On track

1 Sandy wants to check her answer to the sum 197 + 504. What simple calculation would give her an approximate answer?

2 Use rounding to write an addition sum that you could use to check the calculation 739 − 37 = 702.

Aiming higher

1 Fill in the missing numbers.

a) 197 × 9 is roughly … × … which is …

b) 197 + 501 is roughly … + … which is …

c) 301 − 198 is roughly … − … which is …

2 For question 1, what should the units digit of the answers be?

3 Without working it out, pick the nearest answer to the calculation 60.7 × 10.1.
Explain why you chose your answer.

59	60	590
	600	650

4 Which of these answers are clearly wrong? Show how you know they are wrong.

a) 1271 + 851 = 2123 b) 45 × 20 = 900   c) 180 ÷ 20 = 90

d) half of 72 = 35   e) 19 × 9 = 281   f) 227 ÷ 3 = 109

Using and applying

1 Amber goes to the post office to change some pounds into euros. For every £1 she gets €1.5. She wants to change £30. Her younger brother Zak says she'll get €20. Without working it out how do you know that he's wrong?

2 Approximately how much would seven rolls of this wallpaper cost?
Explain how you worked out your answer.

Wallpaper
£7.95 a roll

12 Fraction pairs

What do you need to know?

- That $\frac{1}{2} = 0.5$; $\frac{1}{4} = 0.25$; $\frac{3}{4} = 0.75$; $\frac{1}{10} = 0.1$; $\frac{1}{100} = 0.01$
- How to identify equivalent fractions

What will you learn?

- How to identify fraction pairs that total 1

Example

Each of these circles has been divided into two separate areas.

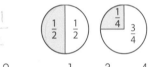

$$\frac{1}{2} + \frac{1}{2} = \frac{2}{2} = 1 \qquad \frac{1}{4} + \frac{3}{4} = \frac{4}{4} = 1$$

These fraction sentences can also be written in decimal form:

$$0.5 + 0.5 = 1 \qquad 0.25 + 0.75 = 1$$

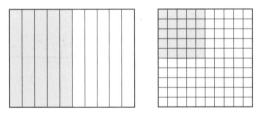

When the top numbers of two fractions add up to the bottom number, the two fractions add up to 1.

$$\frac{1}{8} + \frac{7}{8} = \frac{8}{8} = 1 \qquad \frac{2}{8} + \frac{6}{8} = \frac{8}{8} = 1 \qquad \frac{3}{8} + \frac{5}{8} = \frac{8}{8} = 1$$

Key facts

A fraction that has the same number on the top as on the bottom is equal to 1. $\frac{1}{1} = \frac{2}{2} = \frac{3}{3} = \frac{4}{4} = \frac{5}{5} = 1$

Language

Fraction: a fraction is written with one number on the top (**numerator**) and one number on the bottom (**denominator**).

On track

1 Write a fraction sentence for this diagram.

$\frac{1}{3}$

$\frac{2}{3}$

$\frac{3}{3}$

2 Write fraction sentences for these diagrams.

a)

b)

c)

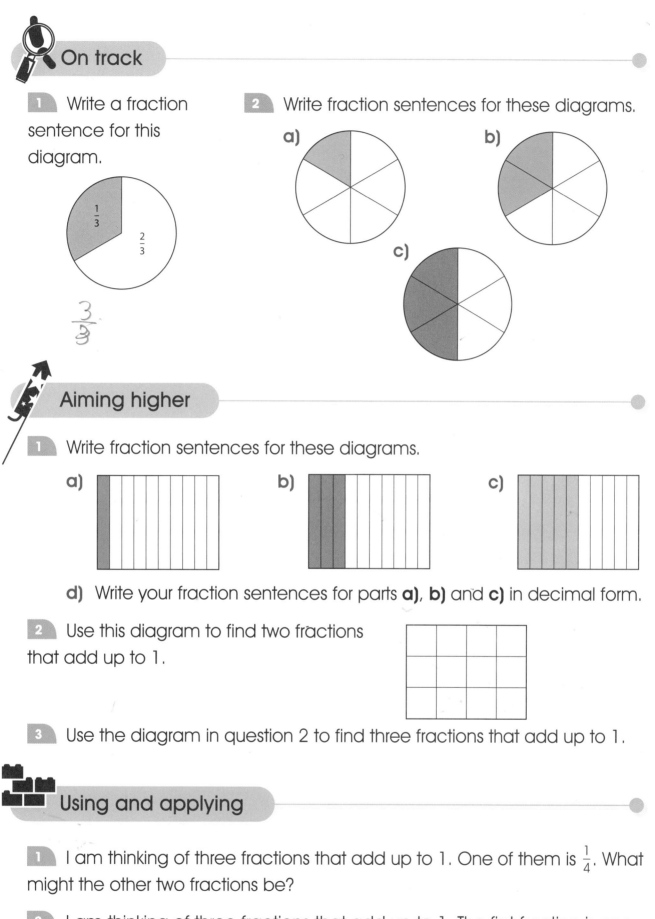

Aiming higher

1 Write fraction sentences for these diagrams.

a)

b)

c)

d) Write your fraction sentences for parts **a)**, **b)** and **c)** in decimal form.

2 Use this diagram to find two fractions that add up to 1.

3 Use the diagram in question 2 to find three fractions that add up to 1.

Using and applying

1 I am thinking of three fractions that add up to 1. One of them is $\frac{1}{4}$. What might the other two fractions be?

2 I am thinking of three fractions that add up to 1. The first fraction is one-half of the second fraction and one-third of the third fraction. What are my three fractions?

13 Mental addition

What do you need to know?

- How to add 1-digit and 2-digit numbers in your head

What will you learn?

- How to add pairs of 2-digit whole numbers mentally

Example

How could you add 15 and 24 in your head?

- *You know how to add a 1-digit number, like 4, to 15. You know how to add a multiple of 10, like 20, to 15. So, partition 24 into 20 + 4 and do the mental calculation in two steps:*

	Step 1	**Step 2**
	Add 4	Add 20
15	$\rightarrow$ 19	$\rightarrow$ 39

The order you add the 4 and the 20 does not matter.

	Step 1	**Step 2**
	Add 20	Add 4
15	$\rightarrow$ 35	$\rightarrow$ 39

Tip!
Decide on an order that suits you and then be systematic.

You could also add 15 to 24, in any order.

$24 + 5 = 29$ $29 + 10 = 39$ and $24 + 10 = 34$ $34 + 5 = 39$

Any number can be partitioned into smaller numbers. Often the partitioning is into tens and units: $15 = 10 + 5$ and $24 = 20 + 4$.

Key facts

The order in which you add two numbers does not matter. You arrive at the same answer, whichever order you use.

Language

Partitioning: splitting a number, e.g. into tens and units.

On track

1 Do these sums in your head.

a) 12 + 7   b) 25 + 3

c) 31 + 5   d) 44 + 8

e) 53 + 9   f) 65 + 6

2 Do these sums in your head.

a) 12 + 50   b) 25 + 10

c) 31 + 30   d) 44 + 60

e) 53 + 70   f) 65 + 40

Aiming higher

1 Do these sums in your head by adding the units digit of the second number first. Then add the tens digit.

a) 42 + 17   b) 45 + 23   c) 51 + 35

d) 44 + 48   e) 13 + 39   f) 25 + 76

2 Do these sums in your head by adding the tens digit of the second number first. Then add the units digit.

a) 52 + 17   b) 35 + 23   c) 61 + 35

d) 24 + 48   e) 23 + 59   f) 15 + 19

3 Do these sums in your head. Notice you are adding a smaller number to a bigger number.

a) 19 + 17   b) 25 + 23   c) 36 + 35

4 Do these sums in your head. Notice you are adding a bigger number to a smaller number.

a) 12 + 17   b) 15 + 23   c) 21 + 35

Using and applying

1 Which method of adding did you prefer? Adding tens first and then units? Or adding units first and then tens? Were you more accurate using one method than the other?

2 Is it easier to add a smaller number to a bigger number, such as 19 to 45? Or, is it easier to add a bigger number to a smaller number, such as 45 to 19. Which method suits you best?

14 Mental subtraction

What do you need to know?

- How to subtract 1-digit and 2-digit numbers in your head

What will you learn?

- How to subtract pairs of 2-digit whole numbers mentally

Example

How could you subtract 15 from 39 in your head?

- *You know how to subtract a 1-digit number, like 5 from 9. You know how to subtract a multiple of 10, like 10, from 30. So, partition 15 into 10 + 5 and do the mental calculation in two steps:*

	Step 1	**Step 2**
	Subtract 10	Subtract 5
39 →	29 →	24

The order you subtract the 10 and the 5 does not matter.

	Step 1	**Step 2**
	Subtract 5	Subtract 10
39 →	34 →	24

Tip!
Decide on an order that suits you and then be systematic.

Another method is to use counting on.

From 15, counting on 5 gets you to 20.	+5
Counting on 10 gets you to 30.	+10
Counting on another 9 gets you to 39.	+9

5 + **10** + **9** = 24 so 39 − 15 = 24

Key facts

Subtraction is the inverse of addition.

Language

Inverse operations: inverse operations 'undo' each other, e.g. addition and subtraction; multiplication and division.

On track

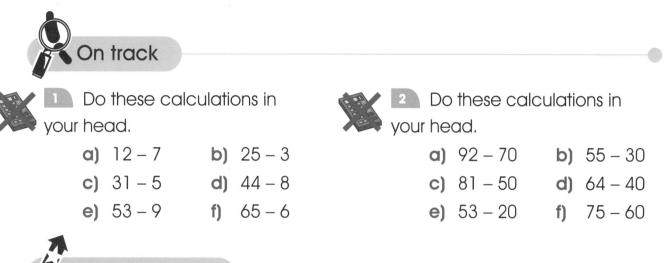

1 Do these calculations in your head.

a) 12 – 7   b) 25 – 3

c) 31 – 5   d) 44 – 8

e) 53 – 9   f) 65 – 6

2 Do these calculations in your head.

a) 92 – 70   b) 55 – 30

c) 81 – 50   d) 64 – 40

e) 53 – 20   f) 75 – 60

Aiming higher

1 Do these calculations in your head by subtracting the units digit of the second number first. Then subtract the tens digit.

a) 42 – 17   b) 45 – 23

c) 51 – 35   d) 64 – 48

e) 73 – 39   f) 35 – 16

2 Do these calculations in your head by subtracting the tens digit of the second number first. Then subtract the units digit.

a) 52 – 17   b) 35 – 23

c) 61 – 35   d) 74 – 48

e) 73 – 59   f) 45 – 19

3 Which method of subtracting did you prefer? Subtracting tens first and then units? Or subtracting units first and then tens?

Were you more accurate using one method than the other?

4 Use the counting-on method for question 1. Did you find this an easier way of finding the answers?

Using and applying

1 There are 68 children on a school trip. 39 are boys. How many of them are girls?

2 In a class there are 29 children. There are 17 boys in the class. How many girls are there?

3 Use these four number cards and the subtraction card to make a calculation whose answer is 22.

15 Written addition and subtraction

What do you need to know?

● How to record addition and subtraction of whole numbers

What will you learn?

● Written methods for money amounts using £ and p notation

Example

You can add and subtract amounts of money in the same way that you add and subtract whole numbers. If there are no pence, just include a £ sign. If there are pence, they are written after a decimal point.

Addition		Subtraction	
£127	£12.55	£350	£10.00
+ £228	+ £7.50	− £275	− £4.75
£355	£20.05	£75	£5.25

When adding or subtracting money amounts, line up the columns carefully.

Key facts

Ten 1p coins are equivalent to one 10p coin. Ten 10p coins are equivalent to one £1 coin.

Language

Total: when asked for the total, add the amounts together.

How much you have left: to work this out, subtract the amount of money you spend from how much money you started with.

Change: to work out the change you should get, subtract the cost of the item you want to buy from the amount you give the shopkeeper.

On track

1 Do these calculations. Lay out your work carefully.
   a) £20 + £10 **b)** £30 + £10 **c)** £40 – £20 **d)** £50 – £10

2 Do these calculations. Lay out your work carefully.
   a) £3.50 + £2.50   **b)** £6.25 + £1.50
   c) £5.75 – £2.50   **d)** £7.50 – £1.75

Aiming higher

1 Do these calculations. Lay out your work carefully.
   a) £27 + £19 **b)** £38 + £16 **c)** £46 – £27 **d)** £58 – £19

2 Do these calculations. Lay out your work carefully.
   a) £3.55 + £2.70   **b)** £6.65 + £1.70
   c) £5.75 – £2.80   **d)** £7.80 – £1.95

Using and applying

1 What is the total of £4.31 and £2.27?

2 James has £6.53. He spends £1.73. How much does he have left?

3 Amber has to work out £9.45 – £1.65. She gives an answer of £7.8. What has she done wrong? What should she have written?

4 Sanjay has saved £4.45; his sister Amber has saved £4.87. How much have they both saved?

5 Amy wants to buy a toy costing £5.85. She has £2.40 saved. How much more does she need to buy the toy?

6 Dan goes shopping for his mum. The total cost is £3.38. He pays with a £5 note. How much change should he get?

7 Peter has saved £14.64. How much more must he save to have £19.50?

8 Amy has £5.79 in her money box. Her gran gives her all her small change to add to this. This amounts to 59p. How much has Amy got now?

16 Multiplying and dividing by 10 or 100

What do you need to know?

- How to multiply 1-digit and 2-digit numbers by 10 and by 100

What will you learn?

- How to multiply and divide numbers up to 1000 by 10 and by 100
- The effect of multiplying and dividing by 10 or 100
- How to scale numbers up and down

Example

Multiplying a digit by 10 makes it 10 times as large, so the digit needs to go in the next column to the left. An extra zero is needed at the end of the number as a placeholder.

$5 \times 10 = 50$ $50 \times 10 = 500$ $500 \times 10 = 5000$

Multiplying a digit by 100 makes it 100 times as large, so the digit needs to go in the next column but one to the left. An extra two zeros are needed at the end of the number as placeholders.

$6 \times 100 = 600$ $60 \times 100 = 6000$ $600 \times 100 = 60,000$

Dividing by 10 (or 100) has the effect of making each digit 10 (or 100) times smaller, so the digit appears one (or two) places to the right of where it started.

$7000 \div 10 = 700$ $700 \div 10 = 70$ $8000 \div 10 = 800$ $8000 \div 100 = 80$

Key facts

Multiplying by a **scale factor** that is greater than 1 makes things larger.
Multiplying by **fractional scale factors** makes things smaller.
A factor of 2 has a doubling effect. A factor of $\frac{1}{2}$ has a halving effect.

Language

Scale factor: a number used to scale other numbers up or down.

On track

1 Copy and complete this multiplication grid.

×	?	8	3
10	100	?	50
5	?	40	25
100	?	?	?

2 Copy and complete these number sentences.

a) $4 \times 100 = \Box$ **b)** $30 \times \Box = 3000$ **c)** $500 \div 100 = \Box$

d) $\Box \div 100 = 24$ **e)** $39 \times \Box = 390$ **f)** $600 \div \Box = 6$

g) $900 = \Box \times 100$ **h)** $\Box \div 100 = 4$

Aiming higher

1 Copy and complete these number sentences.

a) $\Box = (100 \times 2) + (4 \times 10) + 3$ **b)** $630 = 600 + (10 \times \Box)$

c) $901 = (\Box \times 100) + (\Box \times 10) + 1$

2 As you move to the right in this table, numbers are multiplied by 10. Copy and complete the table.

Multiply by 10 →			
3	?	300	3000
?	120	?	12,000
?	?	100	1000
?	50	?	?

Using and applying

1 Change 4000 pence into pounds.

2 How many pence is £20 worth?

3 Choy saves 10p coins. She has saved exactly one hundred 10p coins. How much are these 10p coins worth?

4 Costa Rica has a population of 4 million people. The population of Spain is 10 times bigger. How many million people live in Spain?

17 Written multiplication and division

What do you need to know?

- How to record multiplication and division calculations with remainders

What will you learn?

- How to write multiplication sums
- How to write division sums

Example

Partitioning can be used to work out a multiplication like 13×4:

$13 = 10 + 3 \qquad 13 \times 4 = (10 \times 4) + (3 \times 4) = 40 + 12 = 52$

Partitioning can help division too:

$52 \div 4 = (40 \div 4) + (12 \div 4) = 10 + 3 = 13$

Multiplication calculations can also be set out in a grid like this.

$\times$	**10**	**3**	**13 $\times$ 4**
4	40	12	52

$4 \times 10 = 40$ $4 \times 3 = 12$ $40 + 12 = 52$

Key facts

Some divisions 'go exactly'.
$15 \div 5 = 3$

Some divisions don't 'go exactly' and there is a remainder:

$16 \div 5 = 3$ rem. 1 $17 \div 5 = 3$ rem. 2

$19 \div 5 = 3$ rem. 4 $18 \div 5 = 3$ rem. 3

The remainder can be 1 or 2 or 3 or any number up to 1 before the number you are dividing by. Then it 'goes exactly' again: $20 \div 5 = 4$

Language

Remainder: what is left over when you divide by a number that doesn't 'go exactly'.

On track

1   Use partitioning to calculate 37 × 8.

2   Janet is doing a calculation. Here is her working.

×	**30**	**4**
6	180	24

a)   What is her calculation?

b)   What is the correct answer to her calculation?

3   How does knowing that 10 × 7 = 70 help you to calculate the answer to 84 ÷ 7?

Aiming higher

1   a)   Make up some division questions that have no remainder. How did you do this? Why don't they have a remainder?

b)   Make up some division questions that have a remainder of 1. How did you do it?

2   a)   Give an example of a 2-digit by 1-digit multiplication that you could do mentally. Give an example of a similar multiplication where you would use a written method.

b)   Describe a problem that will give you a remainder that you will need to round up.

c)   What is the largest remainder you can have when you divide by 6?

Using and applying

1   Tomato plants are sold in trays of 8 plants. Amy buys 14 trays. How many tomato plants is this?

2   Tom has 68 football stickers. He sorts them into 4 equal piles. How many football stickers are in each of Tom's piles?

3   Share £94 between three people.

a)   How much does each person get?

b)   How much is left over?

4   I think of a number, multiply it by 3 and the answer is 57. What number did I think of?

18 Finding fractions

What do you need to know?

- That in a fraction like $\frac{3}{8}$, the 3 means 3 parts of a whole and the 8 means the total number of parts
- How to find unit fractions of numbers and of quantities

What will you learn?

- How to find fractions of numbers, quantities and shapes

Example

This rectangle has four rows and six columns. To find $\frac{3}{8}$ of this shape, first work out how many squares make $\frac{1}{8}$ of the rectangle. Then shade three of these areas. Notice that $\frac{3}{8} = \frac{9}{24}$.

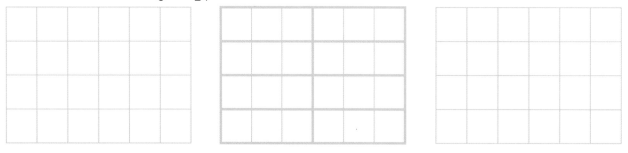

Key facts

To find $\frac{1}{2}$ of something, divide it by 2.

To find $\frac{1}{3}$ of something, divide it by 3. To find $\frac{2}{3}$ of something, find $\frac{1}{3}$ and then double your answer.

To find $\frac{1}{4}$ of something, divide by 4. To find $\frac{3}{4}$ of something, find a $\frac{1}{4}$ of it, and then multiply your answer by 3.

Language

Unit fraction: a fraction with 1 as the numerator (on the top).

Estimate: close to the correct answer. Not a guess. Use approximate numbers in the problem to make the arithmetic easy to do mentally.

On track

1. Draw a circle and divide it into quarters. Shade $\frac{3}{4}$ of the circle.

2. Draw a 4 by 6 rectangle and shade $\frac{5}{8}$ of the shape.

3. Find these quantities.

   a) $\frac{1}{3}$ of 33 m   b) $\frac{1}{5}$ of 45 ml   c) $\frac{1}{7}$ of 35 kg   d) $\frac{2}{3}$ of 33 m

   e) $\frac{2}{5}$ of 45 ml   f) $\frac{2}{7}$ of 35 kg   g) $\frac{3}{4}$ of 16 g   h) $\frac{3}{4}$ of 20 cm

   i) $\frac{3}{4}$ of 32 ml

Aiming higher

1. Find these quantities, converting to the units given.

   a) $\frac{1}{2}$ of 3 m, in cm   b) $\frac{1}{2}$ of 5 l in ml   c) $\frac{1}{2}$ of 7 kg, in g

   d) $\frac{3}{4}$ of 9 kg, in g   e) $\frac{3}{4}$ of 13 m in cm   f) $\frac{3}{4}$ of 17 l in ml

2. a) Draw a circle and divide it into fifths and shade two-fifths.

   b) Draw another circle and divide it into tenths and shade four-tenths.

   c) What do you notice about your answers to parts a) and b)?

3. a) Draw a 2 by 6 grid. Shade $\frac{2}{3}$ of the grid.

   b) Could you have shaded the grid in a different way?

   c) Draw another shaded grid for each new way you discover.

Using and applying

1. Explain how to find $\frac{1}{6}$ of 42.

2. Would you rather have $\frac{1}{5}$ of 30 sweets or $\frac{3}{4}$ of 12 sweets? Why?

3. Which would you rather have: $\frac{1}{3}$ of £30 or $\frac{1}{5}$ of £60? Why?

4. Which would you prefer to receive as pocket money: $\frac{5}{6}$ of £24 or $\frac{3}{7}$ of £49? Why?

19 Using a calculator

What do you need to know?

- How to solve two-step problems involving money, measures or time

What will you learn?

- How to use a calculator to carry out one-step and two-step calculations using the + − × and ÷ keys
- How to recognise negative numbers on the display
- How to correct mistaken entries
- How to interpret the display in the context of money

Example

Before starting a calculation, estimate the answer so that you know what size answer to expect. Then, if the answer is very different, you know you have made a mistake. To correct a mistaken entry, you may need to 'clear' the display. There should be a key on your calculator that lets you change the sign of a number from negative to positive, or from positive to negative.

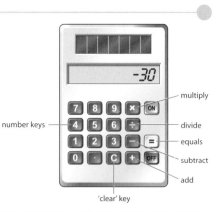

What do all the keys do on your calculator?

Key facts

A number is entered one digit at a time, with the decimal point in the right place as necessary.
Money amounts are keyed without the £ sign or the 'p' for pence, so work in pounds or in pence for the whole calculation.
Pressing the = displays the result of the calculation entered so far.

Language

Key: calculator button which, when pressed, represents a single digit or the decimal point, +, −, x, ÷ or functions such as √ and %.

 On track

1 Imogen used her calculator to work out 123 × 22. By mistake she keyed in 123 × 21 and displayed: What single calculation should she do to show the correct answer on her calculator display?

2 Follow these instructions:
Key a 1-digit number into your calculator. Multiply it by 4649. Multiply the answer by 239. What do you notice about your answer? What happens when you start with a different 1-digit number?

Aiming higher

1 I began with a 1-digit number, then multiplied it by 3, added 8, divided this answer by 2, and subtracted 6 from this answer. My calculator showed the original number! Which 1-digit number did I start with?

2 The product of two whole numbers, both between 10 and 20, is 221. Use your calculator to help you find these two numbers.

Using and applying

For each of these problems, write down the calculation you need to do, write an estimate of the answer and then use your calculator to find the answer.

1 There are 317 people on a train. At the next stop, 39 people get off and 84 get on. How many people are on the train when it sets off again?

2 There are 304 words on a page of a book and 16 words on each line. How many lines are there on a page?

3 Tom's mum goes running to keep fit. She runs 10 km every day, Monday to Friday. On the weekends she runs 20 km a day. How far does she run in a week?

4 Tariq's school holds a car boot sale. It costs people 25p each to get in. It costs each car £10 to be at the sale. How much money was collected from 203 people and the 21 cars who went into the car boot sale?

20 Polygons

What do you need to know?

- How to complete 2-D shapes with reflective symmetry
- The features, such as shapes of faces, of 3-D solids

What will you learn?

- How to draw and classify polygons

Example

Polygons are 2-D shapes made from straight lines.

Sides	Polygon	Name
3		triangle
4		quadrilateral
5		pentagon
6		hexagon
7		heptagon
8		octagon

Key facts

An equilateral triangle has three equal sides. An isosceles triangle has two equal sides. A scalene triangle has no equal sides.

In a convex 2-D shape, all the angles are less than 180°. Angles greater than 180° create concave shapes like the chevron.

Language

2-D shapes: are made from lines that intersect at **vertices**. A 2-D shape with sides all the same length is called **regular**; otherwise it is **irregular**.

3-D solids: are constructed from shapes that are the solids' **faces**. Pairs of faces join along an **edge**.

On track

1 Use isometric paper to draw and label these shapes.

a) an equilateral triangle   b) an isosceles triangle

c) a regular hexagon

2 Use square grid paper to draw and label these shapes.

a) a rectangle, 3 squares by 4 squares

b) a square with side length of 5

3 a) Which two shapes have a line of symmetry?

b) Copy the shapes with line symmetry onto square grid paper and draw the line of symmetry.

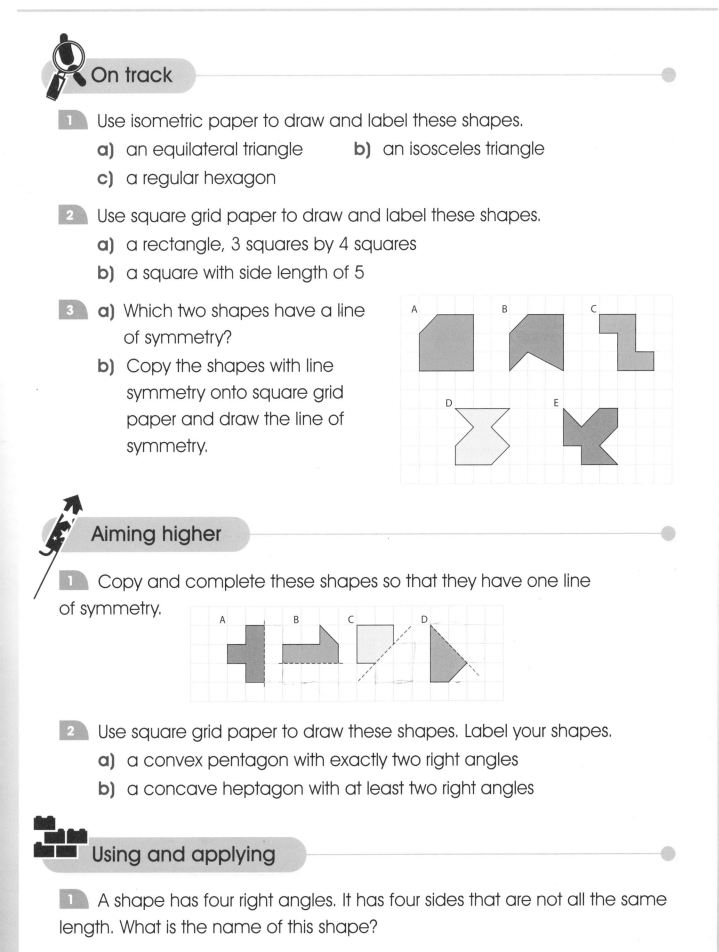

Aiming higher

1 Copy and complete these shapes so that they have one line of symmetry.

2 Use square grid paper to draw these shapes. Label your shapes.

a) a convex pentagon with exactly two right angles

b) a concave heptagon with at least two right angles

Using and applying

1 A shape has four right angles. It has four sides that are not all the same length. What is the name of this shape?

2 What is the difference between a regular and an irregular polygon? Draw two polygons to explain your answer.

21 3-D objects and nets

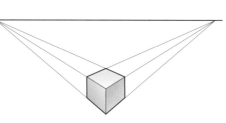

What do you need to know?

- What common 3-D solids look like in different positions and orientations

- How to describe and classify 3-D solids

What will you learn?

- How to visualise 3-D objects from 2-D drawings

- How to make nets of common solids

Example

Drawing a 2-D shape on a piece of paper that also has two dimensions is straightforward. Drawing a 3-D shape on 2-D paper presents a challenge!

To give the impression of three dimensions, a sense of perspective has to be used.

To create a 3-D object from a paper drawing also presents a challenge. Each face needs to be drawn separately, but joined together in such a way that when you fold the net it creates the 3-D solid.

Key facts

Perspective is the way that objects appear to the eye.
Closer objects look larger than those further away, and parallel lines such as railways tracks look like they will meet.

Language

Net: a 2-D drawing that, when cut out and folded, creates a 3-D solid.

On track

1 I am thinking of a 3-D shape. It has a square base. It has four other faces that are triangles. What is the name of the 3-D shape?

2 Name three different 3-D shapes that can have at least one square face.

Aiming higher

1 Anna makes a cube using straws. First she joins four straws to make a square. Then she joins more straws to make a cube.

Altogether, how many straws has she used?

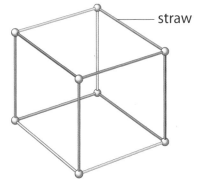

straw

2 Where would you fold this shape to make a cube?

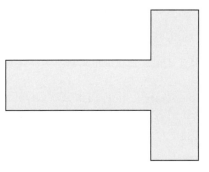

Copy the shape onto square grid paper and draw the fold lines.

Using and applying

1 Take apart a cereal packet (or other empty food packaging) with care. Examine its net. Reproduce the same net, scaled down, and use your net to create a model of the cereal packet.

2 Three 3-D shapes are hidden beneath a cloth: a cube, a pyramid and a cone.

From these clues, work out what each one is called, and its colour.

Clue 1: The cube is in the middle

Clue 2: The pink shape is not on the right

Clue 3: The red shape is next to the pyramid

Clue 4: The cone is not blue

22 Position and direction

What do you need to know?

- The four compass points
- The vocabulary of position, direction and movement

What will you learn?

- How to recognise horizontal and vertical lines
- To use the eight compass points to describe direction
- How to describe and identify positions on a square grid

Example

A grid can be drawn using horizontal and vertical lines on a page.

Horizontal lines are parallel with the horizon.
Vertical lines are perpendicular to horizontal lines.

Movement can be along a row or up a column, or diagonally, and can be described using the eight points of the compass.

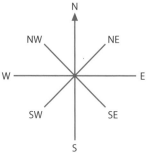

Key facts

A handheld compass points north.

Language

Position: can be given relative to a grid, or described by a distance from a certain point, together with a bearing.

Direction: may be relative to where you are now (ahead of you, behind you) or it may use compass settings (north of you, south-west of you).

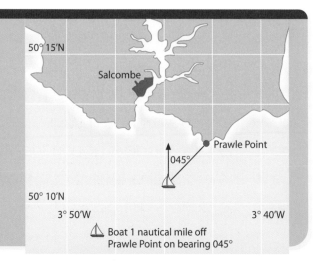

On track

1 Lisa places a counter on square D4. She moves it 2 squares east and 3 squares south.

Where does her counter end up?

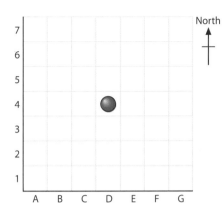

2 Kelly is facing north. She turns clockwise through three right angles. Which direction is she facing now?

Aiming higher

1 Aled is facing north-west. He turns clockwise through two right angles. Which direction is he facing now?

2 Lisa places a counter on square D4 (see **On track**, question 1). She moves it 2 squares north-east, 4 squares south, and 4 squares north–west. Where does her counter end up?

Using and applying

1 Locate your home and your school on a map.

From your classroom, in which direction is your home?

Give your answer in the form of one of the eight points of the compass.

2 **a)** On square grid paper, draw a 10 by 10 map, labelling the columns A–J and the rows 1–10.

b) On your own grid, without anyone else seeing, draw five asterisks in a row to represent hidden treasure.

c) Working in pairs, take turns to guess (by stating the grid reference for one square) where your partner's treasure is hidden.

The first one to find all five asterisks wins.

d) Think about your strategy. Where is the best place to hide treasure? Having found one asterisk, how can you find the others more quickly?

23 Angles

What do you need to know?

- That a right angle represents a quarter turn
- How to use a set square to identify right angles in 2-D shapes
- How to compare angles with a right angle
- That a straight line is equivalent to two right angles

What will you learn?

- That angles are measured in degrees and that one whole turn is 360°
- How to draw, compare and order angles less than 180°

Example

Comparing angles is best done if you align them in some way.

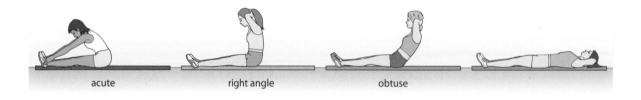

acute   right angle   obtuse

Key facts

An angle is measured in degrees (°)
and goes from 0° (no turn) to 360°
(a full turn).
One half turn is 180° or a
straight line.

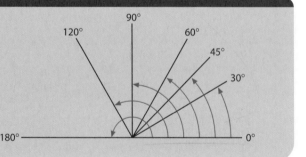

Language

Acute angle: an angle smaller than a right angle.

Obtuse angle: an angle bigger than a right angle but smaller than two right angles.

On track

1 Give two examples of an angle that is bigger than one right angle but smaller than two right angles.

2 Draw an angle that is bigger than a right angle.

Aiming higher

1 Two of these angles are the same size.

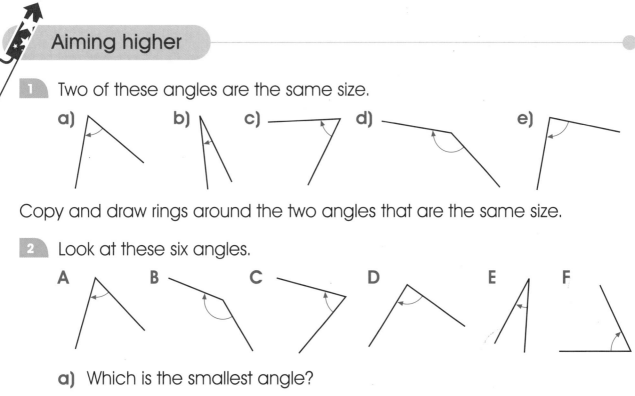

a)   b)   c)   d)   e)

Copy and draw rings around the two angles that are the same size.

2 Look at these six angles.

A   B   C   D   E   F

a) Which is the smallest angle?

b) One of the angles is a right angle. Which is a right angle?

c) One of the angles is an obtuse angle. Which is an obtuse angle?

Using and applying

1 In your classroom, look for examples of right angles, acute angles and obtuse angles. Make a list of what you find.

2 Working in pairs, take it in turns to make a 'walking shape'. One of you stands facing north. The other one gives instructions to turn right or left by a given number of right turns. After each instruction to turn, walk three paces forward.

Try to instruct your partner to 'walk a shape' such as a square, or to trace out a letter such as E.

24 Units of length, weight and capacity

What do you need to know?

- Units for measuring length, weight and capacity: metres (m), grams (g) and litres (*l*)

- 1 kilometre = 1000 metres; 1 metre = 100 centimetres; 1 kilogram = 1000 grams; 1 litre = 1000 millilitres

What will you learn?

- The meaning of 'kilo', 'centi' and 'milli'

- How to use decimal notation to record measurements

Example

The length of this person's finger nail is 14 mm.

Could this be given in different units?

- *Yes, 14 mm is the same as 1.4 cm or 0.014 m.*

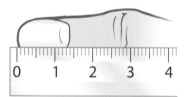

Choosing the right units means you can use fewer digits.

Key facts

Metres (m), centimetres (cm) and kilometres (km) are used to measure length. Grams (g) and kilograms (kg) are used to measure weight. Litres (*l*) and millilitres (ml) are used to measure capacity.

Language

cm: short for centimetre. 'Centi' means a hundredth part.

ml: short for millilitre. 'Milli' means a thousandth part.

kg: short for kilogram. 'Kilo' means a thousand times.

Capacity: a measure of how much something can hold, e.g. how much liquid in a bottle.

On track

1. What units would you use to measure the thickness of a slice of bread?

   a) centimetres   b) millimetres   c) grams   d) kilograms

2. What unit would you use to measure the following?

   a) The distance from here to New York

   b) The length of someone's tie

   c) The depth of water in a puddle

   d) The capacity of a tea cup

   e) The capacity of a lorry's fuel tank

3. Write these amounts in another way, using different units.

   a) 8 km   b) 500 mm   c) 750 ml   d) 4 l

Aiming higher

1. Which is heavier? 2500 g or 3 kg?

Explain how you know.

2. Put these weights in order, heaviest first:

5 kg   500 g $\frac{1}{4}$ kg   1.5 kg   750 g

3. Copy and complete these sentences. Choose the most appropriate value.

   a) The width of a table is about 1.5 / 15 / 150 / 1500 cm.

   b) A drinking glass holds about 0.2 / 2 / 20 / 200 litres.

   c) In an hour, I can walk 5 mm / 5 cm / 5 m / 5 km.

Using and applying

1. Estimate the weight of your maths book.

Check by weighing it.

2. Estimate the height of the window nearest to you, and the width of the door to the classroom.

Check by measuring them with a ruler.

25 Reading scales

What do you need to know?

- How to interpret partially numbered scales
- How to read scales to the nearest half division
- How to draw a line accurately

What will you learn?

- How to interpret intervals on partially numbered scales
- How to record readings to the nearest tenth of a unit

Example

On a ruler, numbering may be shown for each centimetre, but there is no space to number every millimetre.

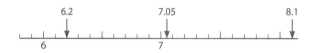

For metric measures, there are usually ten divisions (but check this, just in case it is different).

Key facts

Between two labelled marks on a scale, the divisions are equal. If there are ten divisions, each one is worth one-tenth of the units on the main scale. If there are only eight divisions, each one is one-eighth of the units on the main scale.

Language

Scales: provide a way of measuring physical properties such as length, weight and capacity.

On track

1 What numbers do these arrows point to?

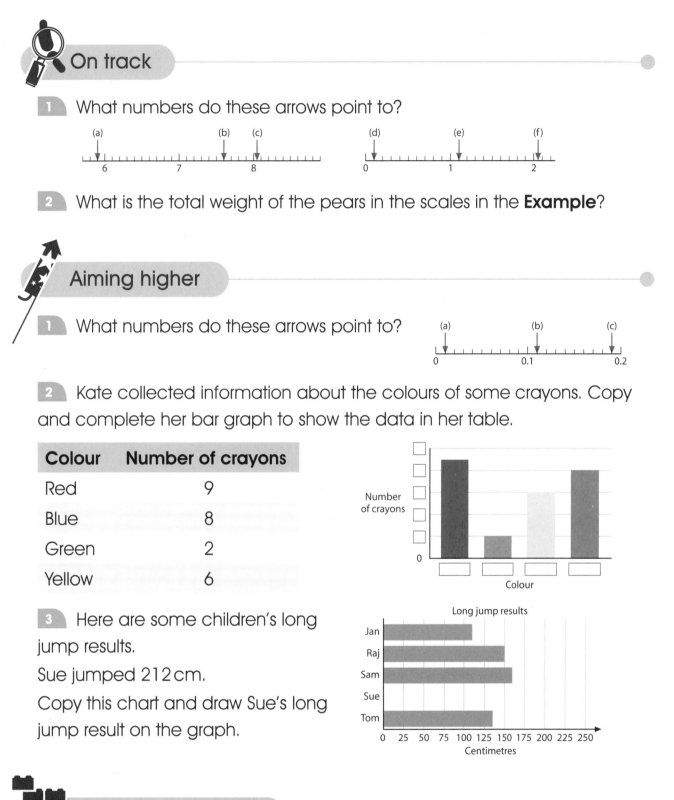

2 What is the total weight of the pears in the scales in the **Example**?

Aiming higher

1 What numbers do these arrows point to?

2 Kate collected information about the colours of some crayons. Copy and complete her bar graph to show the data in her table.

Colour	Number of crayons
Red	9
Blue	8
Green	2
Yellow	6

Number of crayons

Colour

3 Here are some children's long jump results.

Sue jumped 212 cm.

Copy this chart and draw Sue's long jump result on the graph.

Long jump results

Jan
Raj
Sam
Sue
Tom

0 25 50 75 100 125 150 175 200 225 250
Centimetres

Using and applying

1 Imagine a ruler like the one shown in the **Example**. The first part has been snapped off and it starts at 6 cm. How can you use it to make a measurement in centimetres?

2 Use the graph in **Aiming higher**, question 3 to estimate how much further Sam jumped than Tom.

26 Perimeters and areas of rectangles

What do you need to know?

- How to add lengths

What will you learn?

- To draw rectangles and measure and calculate their perimeters
- To count squares on a square grid to find the areas of rectilinear shapes drawn on the grid

Example

The perimeter of a shape is the distance around the edge of the shape.

To calculate the perimeter of a shape, add up the lengths of all the sides.

The area of a shape is the amount of space it covers. The area of a shape drawn on a square grid can be found by counting the squares.

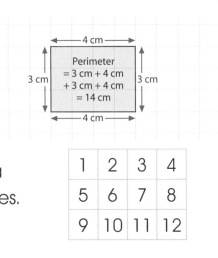

1	2	3	4
5	6	7	8
9	10	11	12

Key facts

The perimeter of a 2-D shape is the sum of the lengths of all the sides.

Language

Rectangle: a quadrilateral (a 4-sided 2-D shape) with a right angle in each corner.

Rectilinear shapes: 2-D shapes that can be drawn keeping to the lines of a rectangular grid.

Perimeter: the perimeter of a 2-D shape is a measure of the distance along the sides of the shape.

Area: the area of a 2-D shape is a measure of the amount of space it takes up.

On track

1   Calculate the perimeters of these shapes.

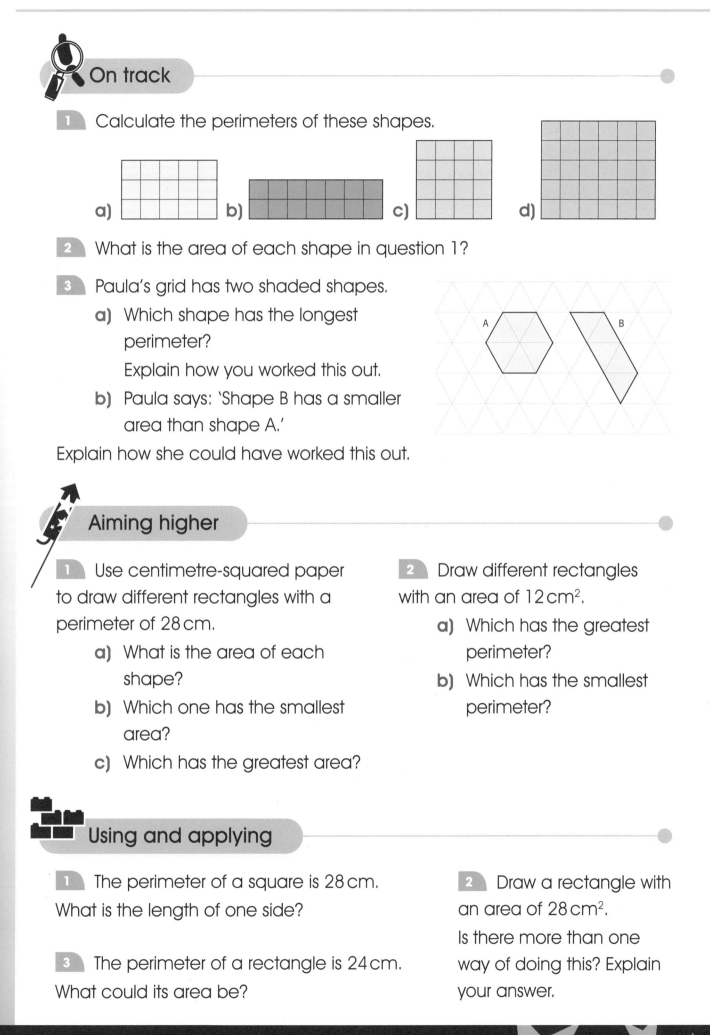

a)   b)   c)   d)

2   What is the area of each shape in question 1?

3   Paula's grid has two shaded shapes.

    a) Which shape has the longest
        perimeter?
        Explain how you worked this out.

    b) Paula says: 'Shape B has a smaller
        area than shape A.'

Explain how she could have worked this out.

Aiming higher

1   Use centimetre-squared paper
to draw different rectangles with a
perimeter of 28 cm.

    a) What is the area of each
        shape?

    b) Which one has the smallest
        area?

    c) Which has the greatest area?

2   Draw different rectangles
with an area of 12 cm^2.

    a) Which has the greatest
        perimeter?

    b) Which has the smallest
        perimeter?

Using and applying

1   The perimeter of a square is 28 cm.
What is the length of one side?

2   Draw a rectangle with
an area of 28 cm^2.

Is there more than one
way of doing this? Explain
your answer.

3   The perimeter of a rectangle is 24 cm.
What could its area be?

27 Intervals of time

What do you need to know?

- How to read the time on a 12-hour digital clock
- How to read an analogue clock to the nearest five minutes

What will you learn?

- To read time to the nearest minute
- To use a.m., p.m. and 12-hour clock notation
- How to calculate time intervals from clocks and timetables

Example

Thursday's maths lesson starts at 2:30 p.m. and finishes at 3:15 p.m. What is the length of the lesson?

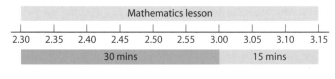

- *From 2:30p.m. to 3:00p.m. is 30 minutes. From 3:00p.m. to 3:15p.m. is another 15 minutes. The length of the lesson is 30 + 15 = 45 minutes.*

The train leaves Nutfield at 8:40 a.m. and arrives at Gratton at 11:10 a.m. How long does the train take?

- *From 8:40a.m. to 9:00a.m. is 20 minutes. From 9:00a.m. to 11:00a.m. is 2 hours. From 11:00a.m. to 11:10a.m. is 10 minutes. The journey length is 20 minutes + 2 hours + 10 minutes = 2 hours 30 minutes.*

Key facts

To calculate a time interval, subtract one time from another. You can't use 'normal' subtraction because there are 60 minutes in 1 hour, not 100.

Language

a.m. means ante meridian (before noon). **p.m.** means post meridian (afternoon).

On track

1 The time is 4:00 p.m. Use a timeline to show:

    a) what time it was three hours ago

    b) what time it will be in 30 minutes' time.

2 It takes 35 minutes to walk from home to school. I need to be there by 8:55 a.m. Use a timeline to show what time I need to leave home.

Aiming higher

1 What time is it on the clock on the wall to the nearest minute? What time will it be 40 minutes from now?

3 What time is it on the clock on the wall to the nearest minute?
How long is it until the lessons ends?

2 What time is it on the clock on the wall to the nearest minute?
How long is it since the lesson started?

4 a) How much does it cost to hire a rowing boat for three hours?

Boat hire	
Motor boats	**Rowing boats**
£7.50 for 15 minutes	£5 for 1 hour

    b) Jack pays £15.00 to hire a motor boat. He goes out at 3:20 p.m. By what time must he return? Explain how you solved this problem.

Using and applying

1 How long do you spend at school each day?
How long do you play computer games each day?
Keep a log for one week and present your results using a chart.

2 What units of time would you choose to answer these questions?

    a) How long have you attended your school?

    b) How long is it until your next birthday?

Make up a question that would be best answered in another unit of time.

28 Tables, charts and diagrams

What do you need to know?

- How to use lists and tables to record data
- How to use block graphs or pictograms to present data
- How to use tally charts, and how to create a frequency table
- How to create a simple bar chart

What will you learn?

- How to decide what data to collect
- How to process your data, using ICT where appropriate

Example

You have an idea that there is a link between height and reach. How would you find out if this is true?

Things to think about	Decisions you might make
What measurements will I need?	The height and the reach
What units will I use?	Metric length: metres
How accurate must I be?	To the nearest centimetre
Who will I measure?	A selection of my friends
Does age matter?	I should include people of all ages

Key facts

If you collect the wrong data, you cannot hope to present any useful results. To collect the 'right' data, you must ask the 'right' questions, and ask the 'right' people.

Language

Frequency: the number of times something happens, like throwing a six on a dice.

On track

1 This bar chart shows the results of a survey of vehicles that passed the school gate between 2:30 p.m. and 3:30 p.m.

What data had to be collected to produce this bar chart?

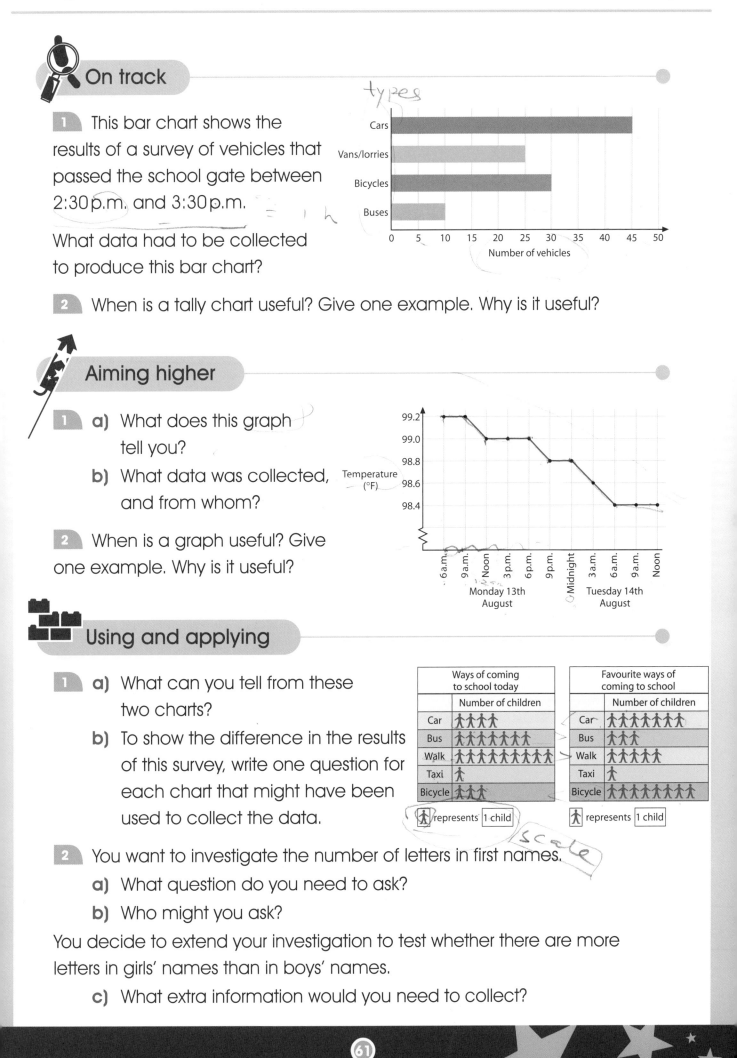

2 When is a tally chart useful? Give one example. Why is it useful?

Aiming higher

1 a) What does this graph tell you?

   b) What data was collected, and from whom?

2 When is a graph useful? Give one example. Why is it useful?

Using and applying

1 a) What can you tell from these two charts?

   b) To show the difference in the results of this survey, write one question for each chart that might have been used to collect the data.

2 You want to investigate the number of letters in first names.

   a) What question do you need to ask?

   b) Who might you ask?

You decide to extend your investigation to test whether there are more letters in girls' names than in boys' names.

   c) What extra information would you need to collect?

29 Scaled data

What do you need to know?

- How to use tally charts, frequency tables, pictograms and bar charts to present results

What will you learn?

- To identify effects of changing step size

Example

These bar charts both show the number of gold medals in the 2004 Olympic Games.

Chart A has the vertical axis numbered in 10s from 0 to 40. Chart B has a greater range and longer step size, with the vertical axis numbered in 25s from 0 to 100.

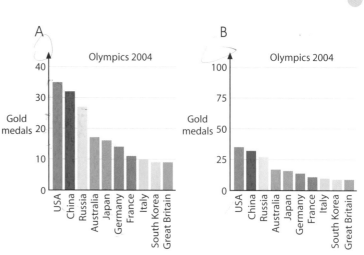

Notice that changing the scale and step size on one axis makes the height differences between the bars seem shorter.

Key facts

How you present your data can have an impact on the message you give. The range of values must be chosen to include the lowest and highest possible values.

Language

Scale factor: a number used to scale other numbers up or down. Multiplying by a scale factor that is greater than 1 makes things larger. Multiplying by fractional scale factors makes things smaller. A factor of 2 has a doubling effect. A factor of $\frac{1}{2}$ has a halving effect.

On track

1. a) Carry out an investigation into the number of letters in the girls' first names in your class.
   b) Record the data in a tally chart and produce a frequency table.
   c) Produce a bar chart to display your results.
   d) Explain how you decided on the range and scale for the frequency axis.

2. Experiment with using a different range and a different scale for your bar chart from question 1. What effect does changing the scale have?

Aiming higher

1. a) Use the Internet to look up the data for the most recent Olympic Games.
   b) Create a bar chart to show the distribution of gold medals among the top ten countries.
   c) Experiment with changing the scale on the vertical axis to exaggerate the differences between the performances of the various countries.

2. a) For one of the bar charts you have produced, look at how you chose the range and scale on the vertical axis. Experiment with using a different range and a different scale. Consider changing the step sizes to 1, 2, 5, 10 and 20 as appropriate.
   b) What effect does changing the scale have?

Using and applying

1. Working with a partner, share examples of bar charts that you have produced. Look for examples where you think a different scale or range would present the data in a better way.

2. Collect some graphs that have been printed in the daily newspapers. Look carefully to see the range and scale used.
Has the data been presented in a true and fair way?

30 Problem-solving questions

On track

1 A piece of rope 214 cm long is cut into four equal pieces. Which sum gives the length of each piece in centimetres?

    a) $214 \div 4$ **b)** 214×4 **c)** $214 - 4$ **d)** $214 + 4$

2 It takes Carol four minutes to wash a window. She wants to know how long it will take to wash eight windows. What should she do?

    a) 8×4 **b)** $8 \div 4$ **c)** $8 - 4$ **d)** $8 + 4$

Aiming higher

1 Write a number sentence to show what calculation you will do to solve this problem: Jill's shopping is £4.29. She decides to pay with a £10 note. How much change should she get?

2 Look at this problem: Jemima buys two coconuts and 0.5 kg of bananas.

    a) How much does Jemima spend on the coconuts?

    b) How much does she spend on the bananas?

    c) Write a number sentence to show what calculation you will do to work out how much she spends altogether.

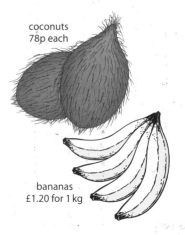

coconuts
78p each

bananas
£1.20 for 1 kg

Using and applying

1 Make up a problem that will need you to use division to solve it. What words will you use to show that division is necessary?

2 Make up a problem that involves subtraction and that requires a change of units before the calculation can be done.

3 Swap your problems for questions 1 and 2 with a friend and solve them. Check your friend's working.